DISNEY · PIXAR
INSIDE OUT

Simply Sadness

By Felicity Glum

Illustrated by Lori Tyminski

A Random House PICTUREBACK® Book

Random House 🏠 New York

Copyright © 2015 Disney Enterprises, Inc., and Pixar Animation Studios. All rights reserved. Published in the United States by Random House Children's Books, a division of Penguin Random House LLC, 1745 Broadway, New York, NY 10019, and in Canada by Random House of Canada Limited, Toronto, in conjunction with Disney Enterprises, Inc. Pictureback, Random House, and the Random House colophon are registered trademarks of Penguin Random House LLC.

randomhousekids.com
ISBN 978-0-7364-3314-3
Printed in the United States of America
10 9 8 7 6 5 4 3 2 1

Oh . . . hi. I'm **Sadness.** This is Headquarters, the control center of Riley's mind. Fear, Disgust, Anger, Joy, and I all take turns helping Riley—only **Joy** doesn't like it very much when I help. She says I make everything gloomy. I guess we're just too different.

I'm trying to work on being more **positive**, so I've found some really good memories. Like the time Riley made an amazing Halloween costume out of toilet paper— but then it **rained**....

Or that time Dad took us fishing—but the boat **leaked** and it smelled like **old fish** and we didn't get a single bite.

That's **not** *exactly* positive.

Here's the **best** memory of all, though—
that afternoon in the twisty tree.

Riley's hockey team,
the Prairie Dogs,
had lost the big playoff game.
Riley had **missed** the winning shot.

She felt awful. She wanted to quit the team.

Mom and Dad came and found Riley. She told them how terrible she felt about losing the game, and they **listened**. They talked about the times they had lost, too, and how bad it felt to let people down. It made Riley feel better to be **sad together**.

That's MY favorite memory, too!

The End

Yeah, the afternoon by the twisty tree is by far my **favorite memory**.

Joy...

Then Mom ordered Riley's favorite food on the whole planet—pizza! They had a big party right there under the tree. It was seriously the best day ever.

It was so **awesome!**

And the memory just gets **better** from there. Out of nowhere, Riley's whole hockey team showed up! Everyone was laughing and cheering, and they lifted Riley into the air!

Mom and Dad were there with Riley. They're always great—they **love** her no matter what. But Riley felt really close to them that day.

But the twisty tree memory is **my all-time favorite.**

Here's a great memory!
This was the day Riley and her
best friend, Meg, built
a **snowman** in Riley's
backyard. They had so much fun!

Oh, yeah! And I love
this one: Riley won a
teddy bear at the
county fair. Look at
that **smile**!

I'm pretty good at making Riley happy, as you can see from her sunny yellow memories.

Hey, no touching, **Sadness!**

Sorry, **Joy**. I just wanted to look.

And I'm not alone. There's Anger, Fear, Disgust, and Sadness.
We all have important jobs to do for Riley. Well . . . all except
Sadness. She just makes Riley sad, which is really the
opposite of what I'm going for.
Sadness and I can't seem to agree on *anything*.

Welcome to Headquarters—the control center of Riley's mind. Riley is an eleven-year-old girl. She is actually the *greatest* eleven-year-old girl, to be exact. Who am I? My name is Joy. I keep things running smoothly around here.

DISNEY · PIXAR

INSIDE OUT

Joy's Greatest Joy

By Felicity Glum
Illustrated by Lori Tyminski

A Random House PICTUREBACK® Book
Random House 🏠 New York

Copyright © 2015 Disney Enterprises, Inc., and Pixar Animation Studios. All rights reserved. Published in the United States by Random House Children's Books, a division of Penguin Random House LLC, 1745 Broadway, New York, NY 10019, and in Canada by Random House of Canada Limited, Toronto, in conjunction with Disney Enterprises, Inc. Pictureback, Random House, and the Random House colophon are registered trademarks of Penguin Random House LLC.

randomhousekids.com
ISBN 978-0-7364-3314-3
Printed in the United States of America
10 9 8 7 6 5 4 3 2 1